DISCARDED
From Nashville Public Library

Property of
Nashville Public Library
615 Church St., Nashville, Tn. 37219

# Bad Boys

by Margie Palatini

illustrated by Henry Cole

KATHERINE TEGEN BOOKS
*An Imprint of HarperCollinsPublishers*

Bad Boys

Text copyright © 2003 by Margie Palatini

Illustrations copyright © 2003 by Henry Cole

Manufactured in China. All rights reserved.

www.harperchildrens.com

Library of Congress Cataloging-in-Publication Data

Palatini, Margie.

Bad boys / by Margie Palatini ; illustrated by Henry Cole. — 1st ed.

p.      cm.

Summary: Two hungry wolves in disguise attempt to raid a sheep farm.

ISBN 0-06-000102-X —ISBN 0-06-000103-8 (lib. bdg.)

[1. Sheep—Fiction.    2. Wolves—Fiction.]    I. Cole, Henry, ill.

PZ7.P1755Bad    2003    [E]—dc21    2002013259

Typography by Elynn Cohen

1 2 3 4 5 6 7 8 9 10

❖

First Edition

for my very good "bad boy"
    —M.P.

Those bad boys, Willy and Wally Wolf, were in trouble.
Again.
And now they were on the run—with everyone
hot on their tails.

Willy stepped out of his granny skirt and chuckled. "Wally, old chum, I do believe we have given them— the slip."

"Yes, indeedy, that was a close one, dear pal," said Wally, coughing up a kernel of corn. "As close . . . as a hair on my chinny-chin-chin."

The two looked at each other and giggled.

"Oh yeah, we're bad. We're bad. We're really, really bad."

Yes, those boys were big. They were bad. . . . And they were also
out of breath. There wasn't another huff or puff between them.
They needed to lay off those goodies and lay low from the law.

But where, oh where, were two big, bad, "wanted" wolves going to hide out where nobody would ever find them?

What to do? What to do? What to do? It was a dilemma, all right.

*"Baa-aa."*

"Do you hear what I hear?" asked Willy of Wally.

"Affirmative," nodded Wally to Willy.

*"Baa-aa."*

"Do you see what I see?" asked Willy of Wally.

"Twenty-twenty," slurped Wally to Willy.

*"Baa-aa."*

"Are you thinking what I'm thinking?" they said to each other.

Those nasty, naughty boys looked at each other and licked their lips.

"Brain ditto!"

Ah, yes! The perfect
hide-out. It was close.
It was clever. And—
eats were included.
"We'll go on the
lam," chuckled Willy.

"Pull the wool over their eyes," chortled Wally.

"Fleece the flock," they both snickered. "Oh yeah, we're bad. We're bad. We're really, really bad."

The boys got out their bag of tricks and went to work. A couple of long-john woollies. Some fluff. More puff. Plenty of mascara and—voilà!

"Willimina and Wallanda," they twittered with a dainty prance.

Two wolves in sheep's clothing! The plan was simple but wickedly devious: lamb smorgasbord!

The boys straightened their stockings. Gave themselves a primp and poof. Powdered their noses. And off they sauntered and sashayed across the meadow.

"Now, remember," cautioned Willy to Wally. "Not one ewe for stew until I give the A-OK."

"No ewe. No stew," agreed Wally.

Oh yes, they were bad. Bad. Really, really baa-aa-ad.

*But*—sort of adorable.

The two were in clover.

Yes, joining the flock was indeed the perfect hide-out.

Not to mention the load of unsuspecting tasty tidbits for the road.
Unfortunately, that tidbit, that morsel, that just one lick of lamb was
getting harder for Willy to resist. He just hated eating his greens.

"This tastes like . . . like . . . *grass*," he said, choking on his brunch of lawn.

Wally picked a blade from his front tooth. "It is grass, you ninny. Just
eat it. . . and smile."

Willy gave a quick floss, for hoofing up the hill were a breakfast,
lunch, and dinner he could really sink his teeth into.

"How do you do, ladies? I'm Betty Mutton, and these are my friends Trudie Ewe and Meryl Sheep. Are you new to the flock?"

Willy batted his eyes coyly. "Well, yes," he answered sweetly. "I suppose you could call us 'two new ewes.' I'm Willimina. And this is my sister, Wallanda."

"We're the Peep Sheep," added Wally.

"The Peep Sheep?" said Betty Mutton without missing a bleat. "You mean, the Bo Peep Sheep? The *missing* Peep Sheep?"

Willy looked to Wally and gave a wink. "Baa-aa-ut of course. I'm sure you've all heard the story. We were lost. So lost. So, *so* lost. And nobody could find us."

"Absolutely, my dears," continued Wally. "Tsk, tsk. It was a terrible thing, don'tcha know. They left us alone! But lookee here . . . now we've come home—"

". . . Wagging our tails behind us," finished Willy with a wiggle and a grin.

Meryl Sheep sighed with relief. "Thank goodness you two are safe with us. Ewes can't be too careful with those big, bad wolves still on the loose."

Wally gave a sly glance to Willy. "Dear me. Haven't they been caught yet? Those boys are *so* baa-aa-ad."

Suddenly, Willy felt weak in the knees. Just the thought of being that close to a leg of lamb dinner after a diet of dried pasture had him swooning in near faint.

Wally fanned the flushed Willy. "You know, girls, I'm scared sheepish myself standing out here in the meadow."

Wally added, "Perhaps . . . we should all jump the fence?"

"Yes," said Willy as he came to. "Let's all jump! I say, why not live a little . . . while you've got the chance?"

The two young ewes were about to take the leap, but tough old Betty Mutton held her ground.

"Just a minute," she said, stepping back. "I knew the Peep Sheep. I grazed with the Peep Sheep. I counted with the Peep Sheep. And you two don't leap like Peep Sheep. There's something very peculiar about you two ewes."

Willy and Wally blinked.

Trudie Ewe suddenly gasped. "Why, Wallanda, what big eyes you have."

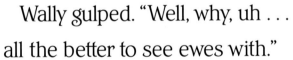

Wally gulped. "Well, why, uh . . . all the better to see ewes with."

"And, Willimina," said Meryl Sheep, staring. "What big ears you have."

Willy gulped. "Well, why, uh . . .
all the better to hear ewes with."

Betty Mutton put her hoof down.
"And what's your excuse for those
lousy-looking coats? If you ask me,
your wool looks too cheap for Peep
Sheep. There isn't three bags full
from either one of you. What's with
you two ewes?"

Willy shrugged. "It's . . . the humidity? You know how wool gets in this damp weather. We can't do a thing with it."

Betty Mutton slowly grinned. "Humidity, hmm? Well, then this is your lucky day, *girls*. I can help you with that. Follow me."

Down the hill went Willy and Wally. With Betty's prodding, they queued up next to each other in back of two long lines of sheep. Wally drooled with delight as he eyeballed the new buffet.

"We sure pulled the wool over their eyes," snickered Wally.

"Indeed we did," said Willy, stifling a chuckle.

The line grew shorter and dinnertime got closer when . . .

BZZZZZZZ

"Excuse me, dear pal, but do you hear what I hear?" Willy whispered to Wally as the line inched forward.

"I do. I do," whispered Wally to Willy. "Bees, pray tell?"

Willy listened.

BZZZZZZZ

"No. Not bees," said Willy.

BZZZZZZZ

"Mowers, perhaps?" whispered Wally to Willy.

BZZZZZZZZZZZZZZ

"No. Not mowers," said Willy.

"Confound it!" cried Wally. "What *is* that annoying buzz?"

BZZZZZZZZLLLLLZZZ

"NEXT!"

Meryl Sheep giggled. "Why—you aren't Willimina!"

Trudie Ewe chuckled. "And you aren't Wallanda."

"Of course they're not," butted in Betty with a hardy snort.

"They're those two nasty, naughty—*naked* big baa-aad wolves."

Willy shivered. "Wally, old chum, I do believe we have been exposed!"

Wally blushed. "Totally, dear pal. Oh me, oh my. Totally."

(And the big, bad wolves thought they had trouble with pigs.)

So they headed for the hills. Of course, there was only one thing those bad boys could do after such a close shave . . .

. . . wait for their hair to grow back—which took a very long time. Those were two very bad haircuts.

Oh yeah, they were bad. Bad. Really, *really* bad.

DISCARDED
From Nashville Public Library